Everyone Loves a
PARADE!*

ANDREA DENISH

ILLUSTRATED BY GUILHERME FRANCO

BOYDS MILLS PRESS

AN IMPRINT OF BOYDS MILLS & KANE

New York

Here comes the parade! What will you see?

Heroes waving to the crowd.

People cheering loud, **loud**, LOUD!

Paper streamers,

rooftop screamers.

Friendly faces floating high.
Unicycles **whizZing** by.
Jazzy kickers,
candy lickers.

Everyone Loves a Parade!*

Flowered ferries, **aaahs** and **ooohs**.
Buzzy buddies, swats and shooos.
Time for lunch,
snacks to munch.

Everyone Loves a Parade!*

Lanterns lighting up the night.

Mighty dragon taking flight.

Pops and **cheers**,

hold your ears.

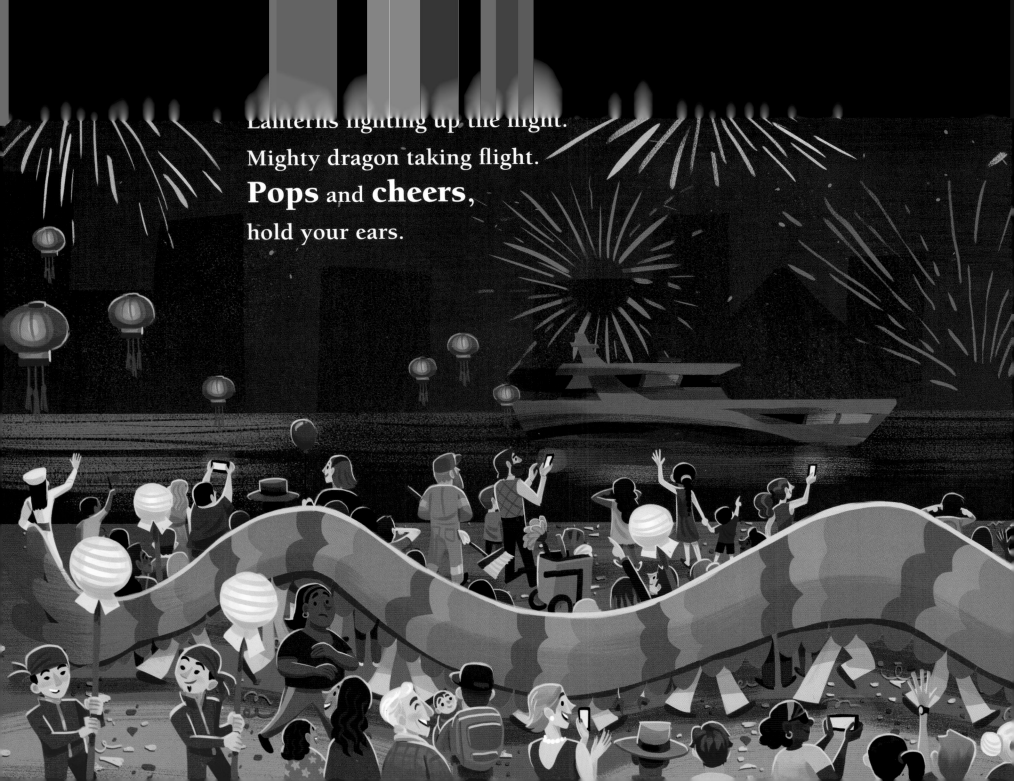

Sports fans line the cityscape.

Cannons blasting ticker tape.

Picture takers,

troublemakers.

Jesters strolling in the street.
Drummers rolling out the beat.
Trinket throwers,
trumpet blowers.

Everyone Loves a Parade!*

Ladies clogging, clicks and claps.
Lucky shamrocks, paddy caps.
Hands to hold,
pot of gold.

Flagpoles spinning, twirls and whirls.
Children singing, boys and girls.
March with pride,
side by side.

Firecrackers! Boom. Fizz. **BAM.**

Stars and stripes for Uncle Sam.

Cones of ice?

Scoop it twice.

EVERYONE LOVES A PARADE!*

Whistles echo far away.
Wishes for another day.
Buses **beeping,**
babies sleeping.

Everyone Loves a Parade!*

The earliest American parades can be traced back to the 1700s. They generally started as simple, but noisy, marches through the streets. Parades were held to mark religious occasions, celebrate victories, or promote something of value. Some of the parades in this book have been held annually for over two hundred years, while others have come about more recently. All parades share a few things in common: they bring communities together, they provide a fun way to celebrate something special, and they are **MESSY!**

Here are some things to know about America's most popular parades.

Heroe's Welcome Parades happen any time of year in large and small towns across the country. They honor military veterans, civic leaders, and noteworthy heroes with a special celebration from their community.

In 1924, the New York City Macy's store planned a parade before presenting the famous Christmas window display. The first parade drew a small crowd and included animals from the Central Park Zoo. Now known nationally as the **Macy's Thanksgiving Day Parade**, the event attracts enormous crowds and features jumbo-sized balloons and performers of all kinds.

The Tournament of Roses Parade was created in 1890 by the Pasadena Hunt Club as a way to show off the beautiful California flowers blooming in the middle of winter. The floats used in the parade compete for prizes and are constructed entirely from plant materials, petals, leaves, seed pods, grasses, and bark.

The Chinese New Year Parade started in 1860 in San Francisco, California. It has grown to be the largest celebration of its kind outside of Asia. The nighttime parade features loads of firecrackers, acrobatic stunts, and the grand appearance of Gum Lung, a 288-foot-long glowing dragon.